# Let's Go, Dear Dragon

A Follett JUST Beginning-To-Read Book

# Let's Go, Dear Dragon

Margaret Hillert

Illustrated by Carl Kock

FOLLETT PUBLISHING COMPANY

Chicago

**Library of Congress Cataloging in Publication Data**

Hillert, Margaret.
Let's go, dear dragon.

(Follett just-beginning-to-read books)
SUMMARY: A boy and his pet dragon celebrate the Fourth of July by going to the beach, having a picnic, and watching the fireworks.
[1. Fourth of July—Fiction. 2. Dragons—Fiction. 3. Seashore—Fiction] I. Kock, Carl. II. Title.
PZ7.H558Le [E] 79–23672
ISBN 0–695–41360–0 lib. bdg.
ISBN 0–695–31360–6 pbk.

Library of Congress Catalog Card Number: 79–23672

International Standard Book Number: 0–695–41360–0 Library binding
0–695–31360–6 Paper binding

First Printing

Get up. Get up.
This is a big day.
A big day for us.

Here.
Help me with this.
Make it go up.
Up, up, up.

And now come here.
Here is one for you.
You can have this one.

See what Mother and Father can do.
Mother and Father can make something.
Something good.
And we can help.

We work here too.
Father and I work.
The car looks good.

Get in the car now.
Get in with me.
We will ride, ride, ride.
We will have fun.

Away we go.
Away, away, away.
What a good day.

Here we are.
Get out. Get out.
We can play here.

Look what I can do to you.
No one can see you now.
No one can guess where you are.

See this.
I can make it go.
It can go up and up.
Get it. Get it.

Oh, my.
Look what you can do.
You are good at this.

We can do this, too.
Work, work, work.
We can do it.

Oh, oh, oh.
Help, help.
Look at us now.
You are too good.

Come with me now.
Come in here.
You will like it.

Go, go, go.
Help me go.
I like to do this.

This looks good.
I want this
and this
and this.

You are a big help.
A big, big help.
Now you have one, too.
It is good to eat.

Oh, look at that!

Do you see that?

Can you do that?

Yes, you can.

You can do it, too.

One, two, three.
GO!
No, that is not good.
That is too little.

Now, here we go.
One, two, three.
Oh, my! Oh, my!
Look at that!
That is good!

Here you are with me.
And here I am with you.
Oh, what a happy day, dear dragon.

**Margaret Hillert,** author of many Follett JUST Beginning-To-Read Books, has been a first-grade teacher in Royal Oak, Michigan, since 1948.

***Let's Go, Dear Dragon*** uses the 65 words listed below.

| | | | |
|---|---|---|---|
| a | father | make | that |
| am | for | me | the |
| and | fun | mother | this |
| are | | my | three |
| at | get | | to |
| away | go | no | too |
| | good | not | two |
| big | guess | now | |
| | | | up |
| can | happy | oh | us |
| car | have | one | |
| come | help | out | want |
| | here | | we |
| day | | play | what |
| dear | I | | where |
| do | in | ride | will |
| dragon | is | | with |
| | it | see | work(s) |
| eat | | something | |
| | like | | yes |
| | little | | you |
| | look | | |